Little ZOMBIE
Activity Book

BARRON'S

ILLUSTRATIONS AND CONCEPT BY PAUL MORAN

WRITTEN AND EDITED BY LAUREN FARNSWORTH

DESIGNED BY BARBARA WARD

First edition for the United States and Canada published in 2014 by Barron's Educational Series, Inc.

First published in Great Britain in 2014 by Buster Books, an imprint of Michael O'Mara Books Ltd., 9 Lion Yard, Tremadoc Road, London SW4 7NQ

Text copyright © Buster Books 2014
Illustrations copyright © Paul Moran 2014

The right of Paul Moran to be identified as the illustrator of the Work has been asserted by him in accordance with the Copyright, Designs and Patent Act 1988.

Additional materials adapted from Shutterstock.com
Haunted House™, House of Terror™, and Spookhouse™ copyright © House Industries

All inquiries should be addressed to:
Barron's Educational Series, Inc.
250 Wireless Boulevard
Hauppauge, NY 11788
www.barronseduc.com

ISBN 13: 978-1-4380-0449-5

Library of Congress Control Number: 2013944925

Date of Manufacture: May 2014
Manufactured by: W06K06T,
  Tsuen Wan, Hong Kong, China

Product conforms to all applicable CPSC and CPSIA 2008 standards. No lead or phthalate hazard.

Printed in China
9 8 7 6 5 4 3 2 1

Beware of the brain-munching zombies—you'll need every inch of that clever, juicy brain of yours to solve these gruesome games, putrefying puzzles, and abominable activities.

Join the zombies in the land of the undead for the most fun you can have with or without a brain.

Squeak!
I am hidden on five pages in this book. Can you find me before the zombies get me?

ZOMBIE IDENTIFIER

Worried your friend might be a zombie?
Use this checklist to find out.

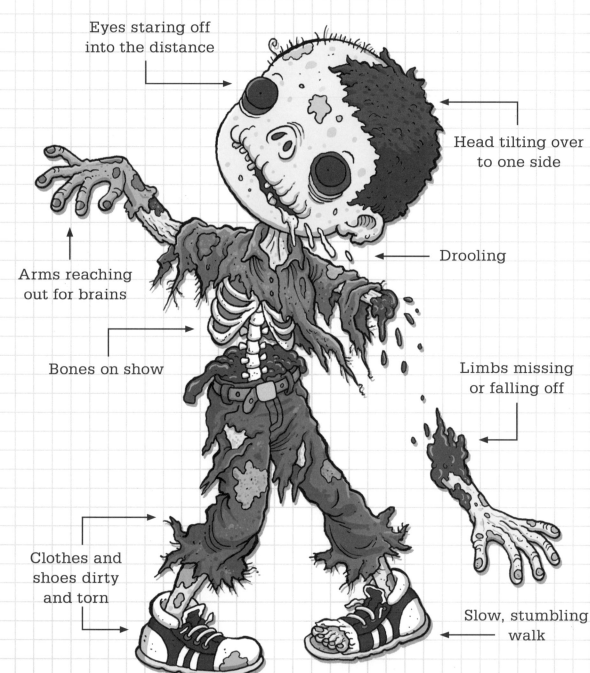

Eyes staring off into the distance

Head tilting over to one side

Drooling

Arms reaching out for brains

Bones on show

Limbs missing or falling off

Clothes and shoes dirty and torn

Slow, stumbling walk

THE ZOMBIE SHUFFLE

The time may come when you need to blend in with a crowd of zombies. Make sure you know the moves.

1. Get into the mindset. Think of your body as something you can't use very well any more.

2. Point your toes slightly inwards. Zombies don't really know which way is forward.

3. Move slowly and, from time to time, stop suddenly.

4. Add some zombie injuries. Did you break your leg? Drag it along behind you. Have you dislocated your shoulder? Then hang your arm loosely at your side.

5. Zombie necks don't have strong muscles, so flop your head to one side.

6. Imagine you can smell tasty brains. Reach out randomly to try to grab them. You're not the most co-ordinated grabber, though, so make sure your movements are clumsy.

7. Don't forget to moan and groan. Moving around takes its toll—let everyone know how unhappy you are about it.

ZOMBIE DISGUISE

You wouldn't really want to look as ugly as a zombie, but you can fake it with face paint. Here's what to do ...

WHAT YOU WILL NEED:
- White, black, red, and green face paints
- Fake blood
- Sponges

1. Give your whole face a white base.

2. Blend a small amount of black all around your eyes to make them look sunken.

3. Dab on a small amount of red and green paint in patches. Blend these using a sponge, so they look like bruises.

4. Rub some black paint over your lips to make them look gray and dry.

5. Drip fake blood from your eyes and mouth. You can also dab blood over other parts of your face to look like you have cuts and bruises.

Now go and show off your fearsome face!

PIECE IT TOGETHER

A mindless zombie has chewed up this photograph.
Can you tell which pieces below fit into the photo?
Check your answers at the back of the book.

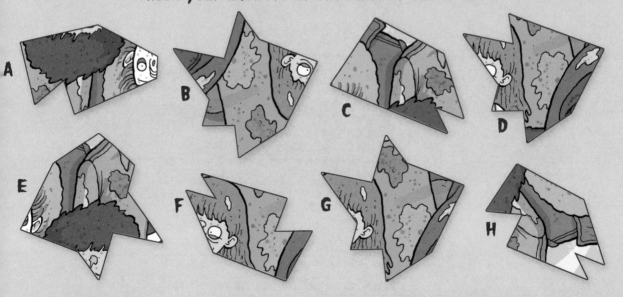

A

B

C

D

E

F

G

H

CHAOS AT THE LAB

The zombies have trashed the school science lab. Color in the scene.

THE RULES

If you want to have any chance of surviving a zombie apocalypse, you'd better stick hard and fast to these rules.

1. Get fit

The fitter you are, the better your chance of escaping a zombie's clutches. Eat plenty of fruit and vegetables, and do lots of exercise.

2. Shhhh!

Don't alert zombies to your whereabouts by being noisy. The quieter you are, the harder it is for them to find you.

3. Travel in groups

Walking alone gives the zombies a better chance of eating you. Make sure you stick with a group of people—ideally, some who can't run as fast as you.

4. Climb high

If you're being chased, get yourself up a tree or over a wall. Zombies won't be able to climb after you.

5. Find shelter

Zombies love dark, moldy, creepy places, so find a bright, open shelter to hide in. That way, you will always see the zombies coming.

6. Check for infection

Check other survivors for bites before you let them into your shelter—they could be infected!

7. Watch where you stand

Zombies are clumsy, but love to be dramatic. Never stand with your back to a window—a zombie is sure to come crashing through to grab you.

BRAIN-DEAD

Do you think you're as stupid as a zombie? Try getting all the answers on this quiz **WRONG**. Succeed and you truly are brain-dead.

1. How long can the brain stay alive without oxygen?

a. 24 hours

b. 4–6 minutes

2. What organ weighs twice as much as your brain?

a. Your skin

b. Your heart

3. How much does the average human brain weigh?

a. 3 lbs (1.3kg)

b. 11.5 lbs (5kg)

4. At what age will your brain stop growing?

a. 18 years

b. Never

5. How much of your brain is made up of water?

a. 10%

b. 75%

6. Which animal has the largest brain?

a. a sperm whale

b. an elephant

PET CEMETERY

The zombies are walking their zombie pets. Draw some zombie pets in the space below.

ZOMBIE JELLY

Sweet and wobbly—everyone loves jelly! But add a few special ingredients, and you can make it fit for a zombie to eat.

WHAT YOU WILL NEED:

- 1 packet of strawberry or raspberry jelly
- 1 jelly mold
- 4 mini brains (walnut halves)
- 6 eyeballs (peeled green grapes)
- a handful of guts (strawberry licorice)

Warning: leave out the walnuts if you, your friends, or your family have a nut allergy!

1. Make some jelly by following the instructions on the packet. This often involves hot water, so ask an adult to help you.

2. Pour your jelly mixture into the jelly mold.

3. Before putting your jelly into the fridge to set, add four walnut halves.

4. Next, add six peeled green grapes to the mixture.

5. Finally, lower in a few pieces of strawberry licorice, twirling them around the walnuts and grapes.

6. Put your jelly mixture into the fridge to set, leaving it for as long as the packet suggests.

7. Once the jelly has set, ask an adult to dip the mold in hot water to loosen it and then put the jelly onto a plate.

Amazing! You now have jelly fit for a zombie. It looks gross, but it will taste great.

SPLAT TO SPLAT

Who's lurking outside? Join the gross drips and splats to find out.

HOW I BECAME A ZOMBIE

Every zombie starts out as just a normal kid. Imagine you have turned into a zombie and fill in the blanks in your story below.

It was just another day at school. I knew something was strange from the moment my teacher Mr. Gormless walked into the classroom. He looked very .... [sick/ gray/ sleepy]. He was dragging his feet and his skin was .... [peeling/ flaky/ scabby].

"I'm sorry I'm late," he said to the class in a .... [harsh/ slow/ moaning] voice. "I've not been feeling well. Open your books and begin the exercise."

I opened my book and tried to concentrate, but I couldn't help looking at Mr. Gormless. He sat down and hunched over his desk, breathing heavily. All of a sudden, he looked up at me with his .... [watery/ bloodshot/ tired] eyes. I kept my head down, but before long, I heard

Mr. Gormless's chair scrape back and his dragging footsteps coming toward me.

Out of the corner of my eye I could see him come to a stop right beside my desk.

"Please see me after class," he said with a raspy breath.

The time flew by and, before I knew it, it was the end of the lesson. The classroom seemed to empty faster than usual—the room had started to smell of .... [mold/ rotting fish/ wet dog].

"Come here, please," Mr. Gormless said quietly. He was clearly finding it difficult to .... [breathe/ speak/ focus].

As I got closer, I could see his .... [skin/ nose/ ears] falling off.

"Sir, are you okay?" I asked.

He turned his head to face me, and I could almost hear his bones .... [crack/ creak/ crunch]. Then, very deliberately, he knocked a pencil off of his desk so that it rolled onto the floor. His fingers had gross-looking .... [blisters/ warts/ scabs] all over them.

"Would you pick that up for me?" he asked. His breath smelled like .... [boiled cabbage/ cheese/ stinky socks]. Yuk!

I knelt and picked up the pencil. My arm was .... [shaking/ trembling/ shivering] as I held it out to him.

"Closer, please," Mr. Gormless said.

I stepped closer, holding my breath. Suddenly, quick as a flash, Mr. Gormless darted forward and clamped his teeth down on my finger.

".. [Ouch/ Get off/ Noooooooooooo]!" I screamed. I held my finger and staggered out of the door.

I could only run for a little while. I soon found myself feeling very .... [wobbly/ stiff/ dizzy]. I shuffled to the end of the corridor and decided to shut myself in the janitor's office. I felt the skin on my face. Was it just me, or was it feeling a little .... [loose/ clammy/ blotchy]? I could also feel my .... [eyes/ teeth/ hair] falling out. Gross!

There was a soft knock at the office door. It creaked open on its hinges. Mr. Gormless stood in the doorway, smiling with his .... [broken/ yellow/ gappy] teeth.

"Join me," he said and smiled an ugly smile. "Together we will turn everyone in this whole school into little zombies!"

Well, what could I do? I joined Mr. Gormless, and together we created a wild bunch of zombie kids. But we're all happy, as none of us have to do .... [math/ history/ science] homework again!

TIMETABLE OF TERROR

Even zombies have to go to school, though there's not much chance of getting them to learn anything. Fill in this school timetable with all the lessons you think a zombie should have.

Subject	Teacher	Lesson
Home Economics	Mr. Stitch	How to sew on your severed limbs
Biology	Ms. Splat	Why zombies continue to stagger around, even though they are dead

Now create your own gross
zombie school uniform.

Is your shirt splattered
with brains?

Are your pants
torn to pieces?

Are you missing
a shoe?

'ORRIBLE ORIGAMI

This scary skull is easy to fold out of paper, and you can even make it talk.

WHAT YOU WILL NEED:
- a large square of paper
- coloring pens or pencils

1. Make a cross on your square of paper by folding it corner to corner and then opening it out.

3. Fold the top corner down, as shown by the arrow.

2. Fold it into a kite shape by bringing the left and right corners to meet in the middle.

4. Fold the long bottom point up so it meets the top of the skull.

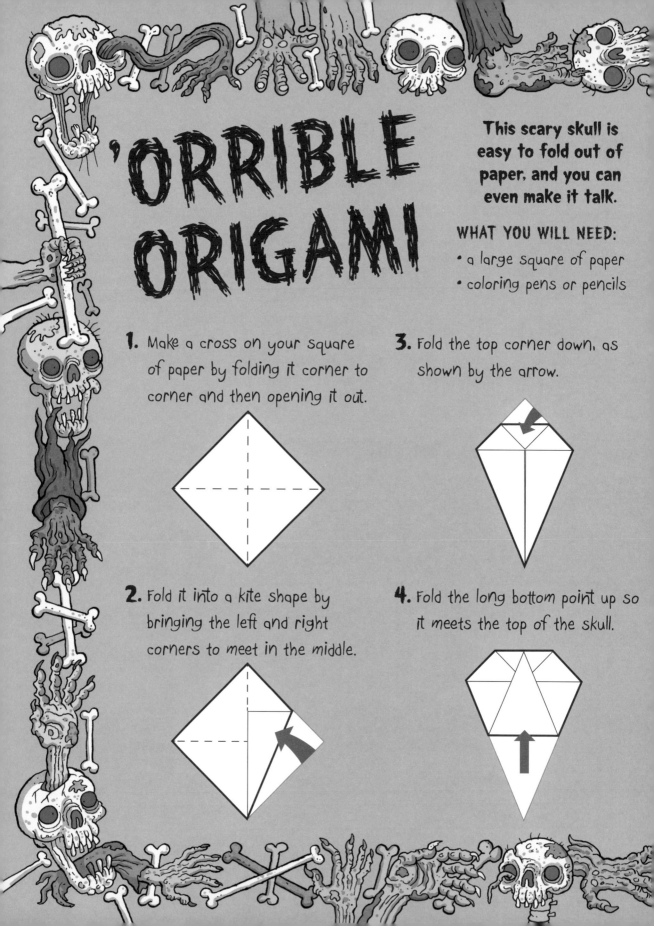

5. Fold the point back down, but leave a little space above your first fold.

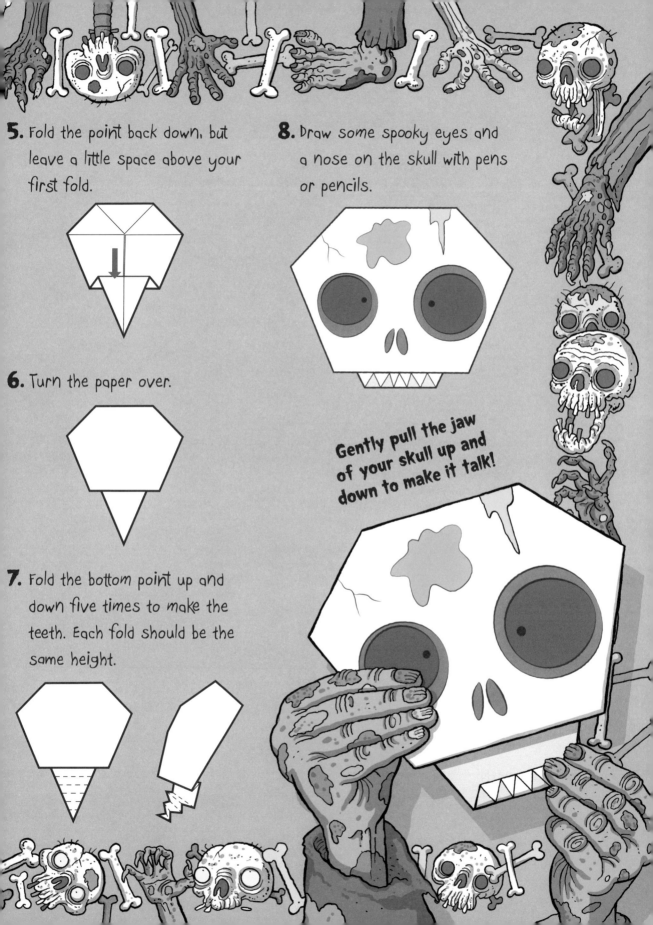

6. Turn the paper over.

7. Fold the bottom point up and down five times to make the teeth. Each fold should be the same height.

8. Draw some spooky eyes and a nose on the skull with pens or pencils.

Gently pull the jaw of your skull up and down to make it talk!

TERRIBLY TRUE OR FOULY FALSE?

There are seven scary, spooky, and sickening stories below. You might wish that they were all made up, but only three of them are. Can you guess which ones? The answers are at the back of the book.

Revolting Remedy

In ancient Roman times, eating the brain of a cat was a recommended cure for a chesty cough.

Mice Slice

If you had bad breath in ancient Egypt, one cure was to cut a mouse in two and place one half inside your mouth.

Rest In Peace

When the wife of an English knight named Sir John Price died in the 17th century, he had her body embalmed (preserved). Each night he slept in his bed beside her—even when he married his second wife.

Deathly White

For several centuries in the past, European high-born ladies would cover their faces with white make-up called ceruse. This horrible mixture of white lead and vinegar slowly poisoned them. It caused hair loss, rotting teeth, and eventually death.

Doctor Death

In the 18th century, a German doctor named Frederik Franheimer decided to make his very own Frankenstein's monster. He would creep out at night, steal body parts from graves, and take them back to his laboratory. He never got to finish the monster, as he was arrested for grave robbing.

Deadly Ducking

Centuries ago, women accused of witchcraft would be tied to a device called a ducking stool and plunged into water. If they floated, they were guilty (and executed). If they drowned, they were innocent (but still dead).

A-head Of The Rest

There is a small, rural village in Argentina where it is said that collecting severed heads will bring you great luck.

WHAT
DID YOU SAY?

Finally—no more trying for hours to guess what zombies are trying to say. Use this translator to find out what they are saying and also to talk back to them.

What they might say to you	
Zomb-ish	**English**
Braaaiiins	Brains
Yoo tastee	You look tasty.
Oh ma arm	Oh no, my arm fell off.
Yoo eye yum yum	Your eyeballs smell yummy.
Whaa?	What?

What you might say	
English	**Zomb-ish**
Hello	Hee-ohh
What's your name?	Wah ya nah
Would you mind not eating my brain?	Woo mah na ee braaaiiiin?
Get lost!	Geee loz!
What a lovely shade of green you are.	Wah luvvy gree

ZOMBIE ME

Imagine what you'd look like as a particularly gruesome member of the undead, and draw yourself in the frame.

DEADLY
SPORTS DAY

START

You trip over your
own severed arm.
Go back 2 spaces.

Your legs are
on backwards!
Move back
1 space.

It's the eyeball and spoon
race, but your arm has
fallen off and you've lost
your eyeball! Go back
2 spaces to pick it up.

You smell sweet, stick
brains at the finish
line—it spurs you on
Skip ahead 3 spaces

If you think sports day is hard, try doing it as a zombie. Grab board pieces, a dice, and a friend, and see who can reach the finish line first.

Your rivals get distracted by something shiny. Skip ahead 1 space.

Your bones get jumbled up in the sack race. Miss a turn while you put them back together.

You fall through a hedge—and find a shortcut.

FINISH

MUTANT MUG SHOTS

Edgar the Eyeless

Give each zombie below a name to describe their gruesome injuries. Be as creative as you can. The first one has been done for you.

Don't forget to color them in!

SCRATCHY SCABS

Here's how to freak out your friends and make some very gross fake scabs.

WHAT YOU WILL NEED:

- a small handful of puffed rice cereal
- a teaspoon
- a small bowl
- 2 teaspoons of golden syrup
- a few drops of red food coloring

1. Put the cereal in a bowl and crush the puffed rice into smaller pieces with the back of a teaspoon.

2. Add two teaspoons of syrup.

3. Add a few drops of red food coloring.

4. Mix together well.

5. Spread the mixture onto your skin, and leave for about 10 minutes to dry. The mixture will still be sticky, so make sure your scab doesn't touch anything, especially furniture or clothes.

Now you're ready to scare your friends!

WOULD YOU RATHER ... ?

Drool nonstop **OR** have your legs on backwards?

Eat a moldy sandwich **OR** brain pie?

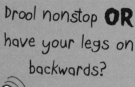

Have absolutely no teeth **OR** be completely bald?

Be covered in scabs **OR** covered in flies?

Play ping pong with your eyeballs **OR** basketball with your brain?

WHAT'S IN THE SKULL?

Doodle what's coming out of this poor zombie's cracked-open head.

BRAINIAC

Think you know everything about zombies? Put your skills to the test with this brainiac quiz.

1. What is a zombie?
- **a.** an undead being that likes to munch on brains
- **b.** a mythical half-fish, half-woman that lives under the sea
- **c.** a horse with a single horn growing from its head

2. When is World Zombie Day?
- **a.** 25th December
- **b.** 1st January
- **c.** 8th October

3. In which country did zombie folklore start?
- **a.** U.K.
- **b.** Italy
- **c.** Haiti

4. How can you get infected with the zombie virus?
- **a.** eating pizza before bedtime
- **b.** watching too much TV
- **c.** a bite from a zombie

5. What is the normal color of zombie skin?
- **a.** pink with yellow spots
- **b.** gray or green
- **c.** bright blue

6. According to folklore, what is the only way to kill a zombie?
- **a.** cut off its ears
- **b.** eat its left foot
- **c.** destroy its brain

Check your answers at the back of the book to get your score and to find out if you're a brainiac.

Are you a brainiac?

5-6 correct
Excellent! You're a zombie expert.

3-4 correct
Not bad, but some improvement needed.

1-2 correct
No good. Back to zombie school for you.

BRAINS
BY NUMBERS

Follow the number key to color in this brain-tastic circus scene.

These twins used to be identical before they turned into zombies.

Can you spot **EIGHT** differences between them?

DEAD ENDS

Avoid the obstacles to escape this graveyard maze.

START

END

WHAT'S IN THE BOX?

Want to gross out your friends? Grab some cardboard boxes, cut holes in the tops just big enough for your hand to slip through, and fill the insides with these yucky things ...

Make sure to give your boxes gross labels to scare your friends.

EARS

(dried apricots)

EYEBALLS

(peeled grapes)

BRAINS

(a cauliflower smothered in syrup)

MAGGOTS

(a bowl of cold, cooked rice mixed with a little water)

GUTS

(cold, cooked spaghetti)

SPLAT ATTACK

Color all the splats that have a dot inside with a black felt-tip pen. What can you see?

Oh no, you silly zombie, you've gone and lost both your arms. Now you have to draw a picture with your foot instead.

See if you can copy the picture on the left by holding a pencil between your toes.

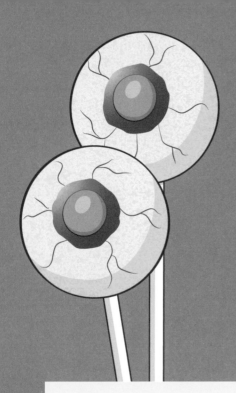

EYEBALL CAKE POPS

Add a dash of fear to a party by making up a batch of these eye-popping treats.

WHAT YOU WILL NEED:

- 1 mixing bowl
- 9 oz (250g) plain sponge cake
- 1 tbsp white icing
- large block of polystyrene
- lollipop sticks
- red food coloring
- small round sweets (jellies or chocolates)
- a small paint brush

1. In a mixing bowl, crumble the sponge cake into fine crumbs.

2. Add the icing, a teaspoon at a time, and mix well into the sponge cake crumbs until you have a firm mixture that can be rolled into balls.

3. Place two heaped teaspoons of the mixture into your hands and roll into a ball. Repeat until you have about eight cake balls.

4. Place the cake balls into the freezer for about 30 minutes.

5. Using one of your lollipop sticks, poke eight well-spaced holes into one side of the polystyrene. Make sure they are deep enough so the lollipop sticks stand up by themselves.

6. Take the cake balls out of the freezer. Poke a lollipop stick into each cake ball, until it is firmly in place. Hold your cake pops up by placing them into the holes in the block of polystyrene.

7. Push a sweet into each cake pop. These make the irises of the eyeballs.

8. Using a small paint brush and the red food coloring, paint spindly veins over the eyeball cake pops. Try adding a red rim around the sweet for very ghoulish eyes.

Yummy!

GOODBYE EYE

These zombies' eyeballs have popped out of their heads. Can you find out which eyeball belongs to which zombie? The answers are at the back of the book.

Ringo

Sally

Marvin

A

B

C

OFF WITH HIS HEAD

Oh dear. Alan's gone and lost his head again, and it's gotten mixed up with other zombie heads rolling around on the floor. Can you help him find it?

Alan's head has two ears, hair, and no brains visible. The answer is at the back of the book.

HAPPY HEAD HUNTING!

SCARY PAIRS

Barry has lost his arms and legs. Can you spot his missing limbs in the junk pile? Hint: his clothes and shoes need to match.

Can you also find
eight loose ears?

THE GREAT ESCAPE?

The kids in this story have stumbled across two zombies. Will they escape? You decide ...

Fill in the spaces with your own words and pictures to finish the story.

THE UNDEAD PRESS

Zombie humans might only be a myth, but these real-life zombie tales from the animal world might keep you up at night.

WIGGLING WORMS

Villain: worms

Victim: snails

When a certain worm is eaten by a snail, it infects the snail's brain and travels to its antennae. The worm transforms the antennae to look like wiggling maggots and makes the snail crawl into the open, where birds usually mistake it for a tasty maggot lunch.

BAD BARNACLES

Villain: barnacles

Victim: crabs

Female Sacculina barnacles love to nest inside crabs. Once inside, the barnacle makes itself at home, spreading tendrils through the crab's body and slowly eating it from inside. Soon the crab will do nothing else than serve its zombie master.

Wicked Wasps

Villain: wasps

Victim: cockroaches

When a jewel wasp injects its venom into a cockroach, the roach will become partially paralyzed and unable to think for itself. The wasp then leads the zombified roach to its lair by using one of the roach's antennae like a dog's lead. The wasp lays its egg inside the lair near the roach. When the egg hatches, the larva (baby wasp) feasts on the roach's organs, munching them one by one so the roach lives as long as possible.

Freaky Fungus

Villain: fungus

Victim: carpenter ants

There is a type of body-snatching fungus that preys on carpenter ants. The fungus infects the ant's brain and takes over its movements. The zombified ant will leave its colony, latch on to the underside of a leaf, and eventually die. The fungus then spreads around the ant's body and produces a stalk from the dead zombie's head that shoots out spores, which lure in other ants.

THE CURE!

Jimmy the zombie is a bit smarter than his zombie friends and has invented the zombie cure. Guzzle down this healthy drink whenever you're feeling a bit mindless.

YOU WILL NEED:

- ½ quart (½ l) of apple juice
- 5 oz (150g) spinach, chopped
- 1 green apple, chopped
- ½ avocado, chopped
- a blender (and an adult to help you)

Combine all the ingredients in a blender ...

Get an adult to help you with the blender.

... then guzzle it down ... wait ... wait.

You're cured!

THE ANSWERS

He's 'Armless! (p. 5)

The correct path is B.

Piece It Together (p. 9)

The correct pieces are B and H.

Brain-dead (remember: these are the WRONG answers) (p. 16)

1. a   3. b   5. a
2. b   4. b   6. b

Terribly True or Fouly False (p. 30)

The false stories are:
Revolting Remedy, Doctor Death, and A-head Of The Rest.

Brainiac (p. 42)

1. a   3. c   5. b
2. c   4. c   6. c

Goodbye Eye (p. 54)

Ringo's eyeball is A.
Sally's eyeball is B.
Marvin's eyeball is C.

Off With His Head (p. 55)

Alan's head is G.